Why Worry?

Written by Eric A. Kimmel
Illustrated by Aiko Ikegami

WEST
MARGIN
PRESS®

Once upon a time there were two good friends, Cricket and Grasshopper. Grasshopper had an apartment in the trunk of a hollow tree. Cricket lived in a cozy cellar beneath a rock.

They were good friends, but different, as you will see.

Cricket always worried.

Grasshopper never did.

One morning Grasshopper called to her friend,
"Hi, Cricket! Isn't this a fine day? Just perfect
for a little spring cleaning."

"I don't know, Grasshopper. I have a feeling something terrible is going to happen today."

"Don't be silly," Grasshopper replied. "What could happen on a fine day like this? Let's have some flower tea. Tea will do you good."

"Yes," Cricket said. "It might calm my nerves."

Cricket shut the cellar door and set off for Grasshopper's house. As soon as he stepped outside, a crow swooped down and snatched him up.

"I knew this would happen," Cricket said as the crow flew away with him.

"Let him go, you wicked bird!" Grasshopper shouted from her window. The crow snatched her up too.

"I'm sorry to have caused all this trouble," Cricket said.

"It's no trouble at all. Everything will turn out all right.
You'll see." Grasshopper waved her feather duster at the
crow. "Let us go, you ridiculous bird!"

AAAAAAAHHHHHHHHHHCHHHHHHHOOOOOOOO!!!!!!!

The crow gave a tremendous sneeze.

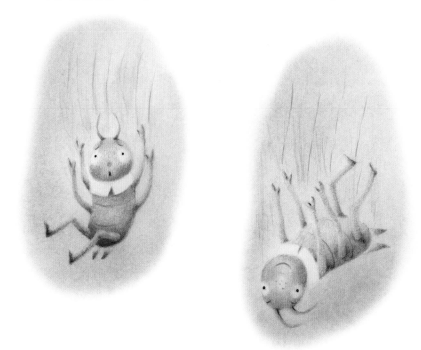

Cricket and Grasshopper went tumbling down, down, down.

"We'll be smashed to bits!" Cricket cried.

"Don't worry," Grasshopper said. "We'll come out swimmingly."

And they did.

The two friends splashed down in the middle of a pond.

"There!" said Grasshopper. "Didn't I tell you not to worry?"

"But I can't swim!" bubbled Cricket.

"Now that you mention it, neither can I," said Grasshopper. "But I'm sure something will turn up."

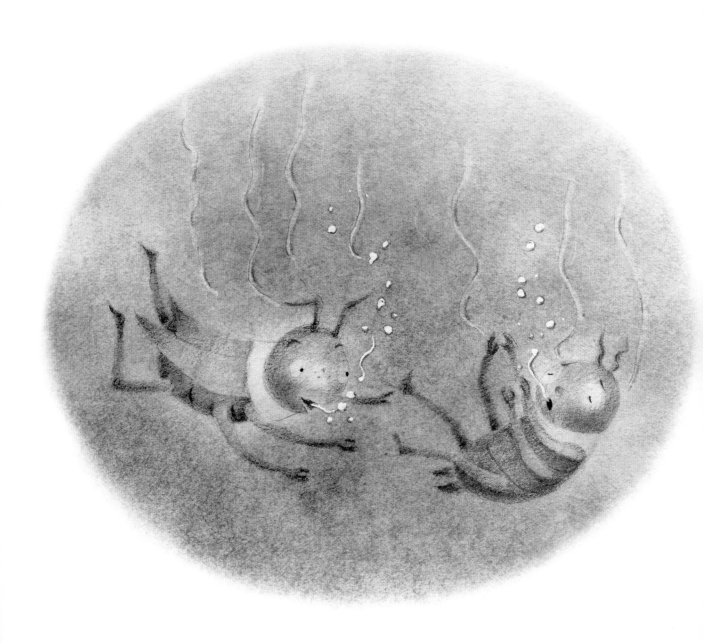

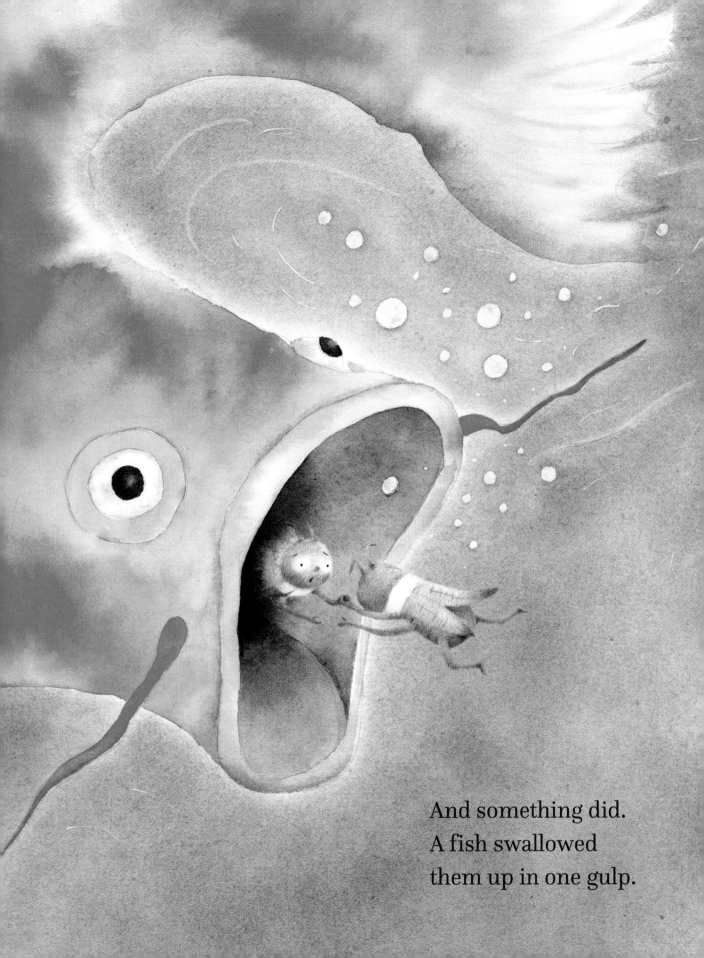

And something did.
A fish swallowed
them up in one gulp.

"It's awfully dark in here," Cricket whispered.

"Musty too," Grasshopper agreed.

Cricket began to cry. "I feel so nervous and upset."

"There, there." Grasshopper put her arms around Cricket. "Have a good cry. You'll feel better."

Cricket moaned. "We'll be trapped here forever."

"We'll get out," Grasshopper said. "We just have to wait a bit."

So they waited.

   And waited.

      And waited.

Suddenly, they felt a tremendous tossing and shaking.

"What's going on?" cried Cricket.

"We'll find out soon enough," said Grasshopper.

Indeed they did.

The fish was caught on the end of a hook. It thrashed and leaped, but it was no use. The fish was lifted out of the water.

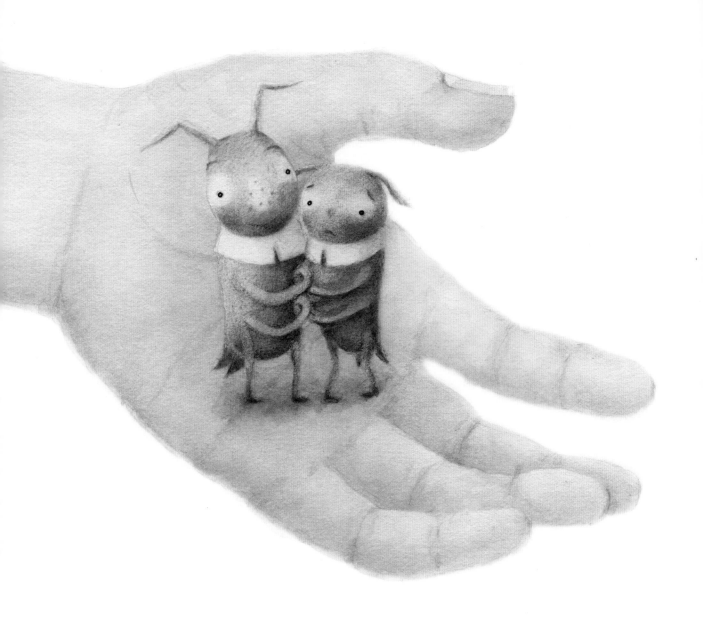

They saw a flash of light, followed by voices.

"Hey! There are bugs inside this fish!"

"Don't let them get away!" A hand thrust Cricket and Grasshopper into an empty jar. A lid closed over them.

"I don't feel well," said Cricket.

Grasshopper jumped up and down.
"Hello out there! Could you give us some air?"

The lid began to turn.

"Thank goodness!" said Cricket.

Before they could say a word, the two friends were pulled from the jar, shoved into a plastic bag, and tied to the tail of a kite.

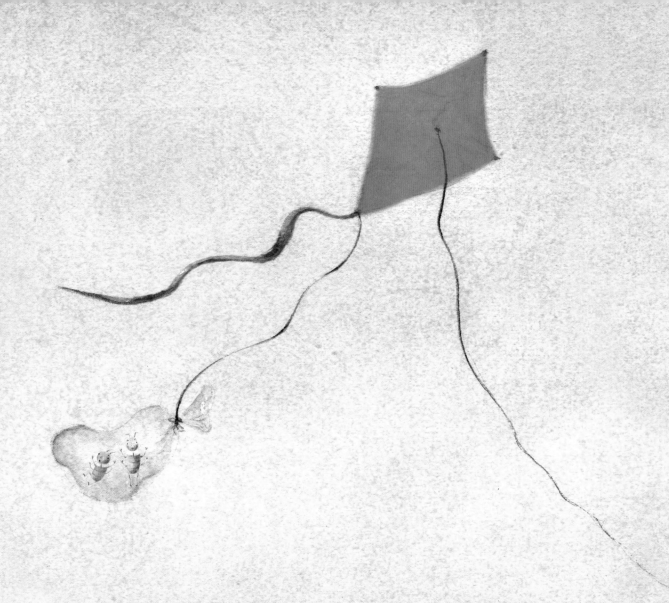

The kite lifted off the ground.
Cricket shut his eyes tight.

"Oh, dear!" Cricket moaned as the kite rose higher and higher. "I knew something terrible was going to happen. I should have stayed home. "

"Now, now," Grasshopper said. "It's not so bad. We're getting to see the world. And when we get home, we'll have so many adventures to talk about."

"We'll never get home," said Cricket.
He began to cry.

"Don't cry, Cricket. Look how high we are!" said Grasshopper. "We're above the treetops. The pond looks like a drop of dew. Oh Cricket, open your eyes! It's wonderful!"

"I think I'm going to throw up," said Cricket.

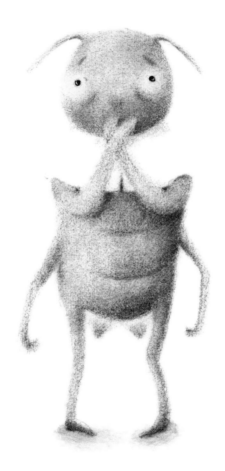

A gust of wind caught the kite. The string snapped. The kite sailed up, up, up.

Above the trees.

Above the clouds.

Cricket shrieked with fright.

But Grasshopper wasn't worried.

"I love flying. Don't you, Cricket?"

Cricket didn't answer. His eyes were clamped shut.

Time passed. The kite stopped moving. Cricket opened his eyes. They were wrapped around a branch. There was something familiar about the tree and the rock beside it.

Cricket jumped for joy. "Look where we are! We're HOME!"

Grasshopper sighed. "I know."

"You don't sound happy about it," Cricket said.

"It is nice to be home," Grasshopper replied. "But I was having such a wonderful time on our adventure that I hoped it might last a little longer."

"I never thought I'd see home again," Cricket said.

Grasshopper took his hand. "Don't you see? You didn't have to worry. Now let's climb down and have our cup of tea."

"I'd like that," Cricket said. "But..."

"But what?"

"You don't think it will be too hot, do you?"

"Oh, Cricket!" Grasshopper laughed. "You don't have to worry!"

And do you know? It was just right.

Children and Worry

Just like Cricket, children worry about many things. They worry about conflicts with parents, siblings, or friends, bullying, and life changes like divorce, moving, or loss of a loved one. They also have fears about not knowing how to handle future situations like schoolwork or a new activity. Children can't control events in their lives and often don't have all the information about what is happening to them. This can increase anxiety.

Some level of worry is normal for everyone. Children, however, can show intense feelings of worry and fear in a number of obvious and subtle ways. They may act out, crying, throwing tantrums, or refusing to follow directions. They may express more subtle signs like complaining of headaches or stomachaches, avoiding stressful situations, or isolating themselves with books or video games.

Here are some ways to help children (and Crickets) deal with their worries:

* Reassure them that there are sometimes good reasons to have fear and concern. Parents can provide reassurance by saying, "We're here. Talk to us. We can help." Children can also say to themselves, "Be brave today."

* Help them reframe their worries into positives about themselves and their new situation by saying, "You are loved. You are safe. This fear will pass."

* Focus on the excitement of a new adventure and their ability to manage the new situation. Parents can say, "Channel your superpower!"

* Roleplay or rehearse a future situation so that it feels less scary and unknown. Parents might say, "Imagine yourself in that situation. Close your eyes. See yourself as powerful and courageous."

* If there is a conflict with a friend, encourage them to talk about it and help them develop an action plan. Say, "This might be scary and difficult, but talking it through is a good way to fix it."

* Offer relaxation techniques to help them learn to calm themselves. Parents might say, "Close your eyes. Relax. Breathe slowly. See yourself in a happy place."

* In some situations, adults may need to intervene and advocate for a child when the child cannot. For example, if a child is bullied, parents might say, "This is not right. I am going to help you through this. I am going to take charge. I will handle this for you and with you."

—Drs. Gayle and Mike Klaybor,
psychotherapists

Text © 2019 by Eric A. Kimmel
Illustrations © 2019 by Aiko Ikegami

Edited by Michelle McCann

Library of Congress Cataloging-in-
Publication Data is on file.

ISBN 9781513262000 (hardbound)
ISBN 9781513262017 (e-book)

Printed in China
22 21 20 19 1 2 3 4 5

Published by West Margin Press®

WEST
MARGIN
PRESS®

WestMarginPress.com

Proudly distributed by
Ingram Publisher Services

WEST MARGIN PRESS
Publishing Director: Jennifer Newens
Marketing Manager: Angela Zbornik
Editor: Olivia Ngai
Design & Production: Rachel Lopez Metzger